Touchdown! Dear Dragon

by Margaret Hillert
Illustrated by David Schimmell

NORWOOD HOUSE PRESS

DEAR CAREGIVER,

The *Beginning-to-Read* series is a carefully written collection of classic readers you may remember from your own childhood. Each book features text comprised of common sight words to provide your child ample practice reading the words that appear most frequently in written text. The many additional details in the pictures enhance the story and offer the opportunity for you to help your child expand oral language and develop comprehension.

Begin by reading the story to your child, followed by letting him or her read familiar words and soon your child will be able to read the story independently. At each step of the way, be sure to praise your reader's efforts to build his or her confidence as an independent reader. Discuss the pictures and encourage your child to make connections between the story and his or her own life. At the end of the story, you will find reading activities and a word list that will help your child practice and strengthen beginning reading skills.

Above all, the most important part of the reading experience is to have fun and enjoy it!

Shannon Cannon

Shannon Cannon,
Literacy Consultant

Norwood House Press • P.O. Box 316598 • Chicago, Illinois 60631
For more information about Norwood House Press please visit our website at *www.norwoodhousepress.com* or call 866-565-2900.

Text copyright ©2009 by Margaret Hillert. Illustrations and cover design copyright ©2009 by Norwood House Press, Inc. All rights reserved. No part of this book may be reproduced or utilized in any form or by any means without written permission from the publisher.
Designer: The Design Lab

LIBRARY OF CONGRESS CATALOGING-IN-PUBLICATION DATA
Hillert, Margaret.
  Touchdown! Dear dragon / by Margaret Hillert ; illustrated by David Schimmell.
    p. cm. — (A beginning-to-read book)
  Summary: "A boy and his pet dragon meet up with their friends and play football"—Provided by publisher.
  ISBN-13: 978-1-59953-296-7 (library edition : alk. paper)
  ISBN-10: 1-59953-296-4 (library edition : alk. paper) [1.
Dragons—Fiction. 2. Football—Fiction.] I. Schimmell, David, ill. II.
Title.
PZ7.H558To 2009
[E]—dc22   2008035971

Manufactured in the United States of America.

We can get up now.
We will find friends to play with.
We will have fun.

Here. Here.
Come here and eat.
It will help you play the game.

Yes, yes.
I like this, and it is good for me.
It will help my game.

I have to put this on.
I see that you have one, too.
That is good.

Now we can go.
We will look for friends.

Look here.
Here is the spot.
We can play here.

Now I have to do this so I can play.

Come on.
Come on.
Run, run, run.

Here I am.
I want to play, too.

Here it is.
Get the ball.
Now go with it.
Run, run, run.

I have it.
I have it.
And here I go.

Oh, NO!
Not that way.
NOT THAT WAY!

Oh, oh.
This is not good.

GO, GO, GO!

I did it!
I did it!

Yes, you were so good.
And you are a good friend.
But I have to go now.

Here you are with me.
And here I am with you.
Oh, what a fun game, dear dragon.

The following activities support the findings of the National Reading Panel that determined the most effective components for reading instruction are: Phonemic Awareness, Phonics, Vocabulary, Fluency, and Text Comprehension.

Phonemic Awareness: The /o͝o/ sound

Oddity Task: Say the **/o͝o/** sound (foot) for your child. Ask your child to say the word that has the **/o͝o/** sound in the following word groups:

foot, zoom, moon   goose, good, goat   zoo, boo, hook

cool, cook, coop   nook, noon, none   soon, spoon, soot

lop, loop, look   book, boot, boom

Phonics: The o͝o spelling

1. Make two columns on a blank sheet of paper and draw a simple illustration of a foot and a moon (one object at the top of each column).

2. Write the following words on separate index cards:

cool	soon	hook	hood	book	school
food	wood	good	moose	hoop	cookie
look	stood	zoo	loop	boot	soot

3. Ask your child to read each word and place the card under the column heading that represents the **/o͝o/** spelling in the word.

   Answers:

   foot: hook, hood, book, wood, good, cookie, look, stood, soot

   moon: cool, soon, school, food, moose, hoop, zoo, loop, boot

4. Ask your child to read each list of words.

Vocabulary: Compound Words

1. Explain to your child that sometimes two words can be put together to make a new word. These are called compound words. The story concept has two compound words: **football** and **touchdown**.

2. Write down the following words on separate pieces of paper:

ground	eye	head	mate	cut	hang	band
key	skin	quarter	end	play	ball	fore
team	hair	out	board	pig	back	week

3. Help your child move the pieces of paper around to form compound words.

Possible answers: playground, eyeball, forehead, teammate, haircut, hangout, headband, keyboard, pigskin, quarterback, weekend

Fluency: Shared Reading

1. Reread the story to your child at least two more times while your child tracks the print by running a finger under the words as they are read. Ask your child to read the words he or she knows with you.

2. Reread the story taking turns by alternating readers of sentences or pages.

Text Comprehension: Discussion Time

1. Ask your child to retell the sequence of events in the story.

2. To check comprehension, ask your child the following questions:
   - Why did the boy and the dragon put on helmets?
   - Why did the kids yell at the boy on pages 18-19? How do you think it made him feel?
   - If a teammate made a mistake in a game, how would you show good sportsmanship?

WORD LIST

Touchdown! Dear Dragon **uses the 58 words listed below.**
This list can be used to practice reading the words that appear in the text.
You may wish to write the words on index cards and use them to help your
child build automatic word recognition. Regular practice with these words
will enhance your child's fluency in reading connected text.

a	find	like	run	want
am	for	look		way
and	friend(s)		see	we
are	fun	me	so	were
		my	spot	what
ball	game			will
but	get	no	that	with
	go	not	the	
can	good	now	this	yes
come			to	you
	have	oh	too	
dear	help	on		
did	here	one	up	
do				
dragon	I	play		
	is	put		
eat	it			

ABOUT THE AUTHOR   Margaret Hillert has written over 80 books for
children who are just learning to read. Her books
have been translated into many different languages and over a million children
throughout the world have read her books. She first started writing poetry as
a child and has continued to write for children and adults throughout her life. A
first grade teacher for 34 years, Margaret is now retired from teaching and lives in
Michigan where she likes to write, take walks in the morning, and care for her three cats.

Photograph by Glenna Washburn

ABOUT THE ADVISER   Shannon Cannon contributed the activities pages that appear in
this book. Shannon serves as a literacy consultant and provides
staff development to help improve reading instruction. She is a frequent presenter at educational
conferences and workshops. Prior to this she worked as an elementary school teacher and as
president of a curriculum publishing company.